Amelia's

MOST
UNFORGETTABLE
EMBARRASSING
MOMENTS

by Marissa Moss
(except all embarrassment is entirely
amelia's!)

TOP
SECRET

Blush-ometer-
DANGER!! →
WAAAAY IN
THE RED ZONE!

Simon & Schuster Books for Young Readers
New York   London   Toronto   Sydney

CAUTION: CONTENTS UNDER PRESSURE! →

SAYING STUPID THINGS COULD BE HAZARDOUS TO YOUR HEALTH!

I thought being in middle school meant you were finally beyond stupid, embarrassing moments. Like you're smart enough NOT to think "adept" means "inept" (just the opposite!) or that the plural of "spaghetti" is "spaghettis" or that "potato" is spelled like it's part of a foot ("potatoe"). I thought at a certain age you outgrew that kind of dumbness, and stupid things didn't come out of your mouth anymore.

Before Middle School ↓

During Middle School ↓

Duh— I dunno.

Doesn't "flummox" mean a flannel ox?

Sure sounds like it.

Hmmm, flum + ox = flummox. That's it — a sick ox, one with the flu, right?

Of course, it's entirely plausible that unforeseen events will create inexplicable consequences.

Can't you tell I know EXACTLY what I'm saying?

If that were true, this would be a VERY different kind of notebook. Unfortunately I've discovered you're never too old to put your foot in your mouth.

Or to embarrass yourself in some other horrible way. Though with me it's things I say that seem to be the worst. Sometimes I want to rewind time so I can NOT say how much I played with troll dolls when I was little. Who wants to admit to that? What possessed me to blurt that out to a complete stranger next to me in line at the cafeteria. What was I thinking?!!

It's all the hairnet lady's fault. Her blue hair reminded me of my favorite troll, Bluebelly. →

She looked like a troll! ←

Try the meatloaf today. It'll stick to your ribs.

And she talked like a troll!

So this notebook, which started out as a middle school journal of all my amazing middle school achievements, is instead a safe place to hide all the things I wish WISH WISH had never happened. If I put them down on paper, maybe I'll get them out of my head and I won't blush just thinking of them all the time.

Then I can focus on the good parts of me in middle school.

Amelia's Embarrassing
HEY!
Oops! sorry!
walking into an occupied stall (or being walked in on)
Did I step in something?
EWWW! GROSS!
tracking dog poop into a classroom
Um, I'll just keep my books today.
I don't need a locker.
strategically placed object to hide awkward evidence
spilling milk or juice and having to walk around with a suspicious stain all day
You forgot your lunch today.
I brought it for you.
Um, thanks.
She's not really my mom, just a nice neighbor.
being seen with your mom at school

Moments Hall of Fame

Still, all in all, middle school is a BIG improvement over Little Kid School (or elementary school, I should say). And today our science teacher, Ms. Reilly, said something that made it even better.

I don't know about the bonding part. There are plenty of kids in this class I DON'T want to know any better than I already do. But the rest sounds good. So long as I don't have to share a room with someone who snores, burps, farts a lot, or talks in their sleep. And so long as I DON'T have to sit next to someone on the bus who gets carsick or sings loudly off-key. In other words, so long as I don't have to travel with anyone like my sister, Cleo.

KIDS TO BE AVOIDED — ESPECIALLY AS PARTNERS FOR ANY KIND OF PROJECT

I like Ms. Reilly. She's a good teacher. — for one 45-minute period. What will it be like spending ③ whole days with her? Maybe too much of a good thing.

She's the kind of enthusiastic teacher who is so excited by what she's talking about, she thinks you must be too—so before you know it, you're hearing details about stuff you never wanted to know.

The first few minutes, it's fascinating. Then it's bearable. Then for the last 10 minutes it's too much — your brain is overflowing.

This is a perfect example of Fibonacci numbers. You don't count the bracts but the spirals winding around the pinecone — clockwise, counterclockwise, it doesn't matter. You'll end up with Fibonacci numbers. Every time. Every pinecone. How does nature do it? Is Mother Nature a mathematician?

Now you ask, what ARE Fibonacci numbers? Let me explain...

← MORE Fibonacci numbers →

I'm NOT asking! I'm too busy counting spirals, losing track, and counting all over again.

We won't just be bonding with each other — we'll be bonding with our teacher. Good thing this field trip isn't led by Mr. Lambaste, my evil English teacher. Ms. Reilly may talk a lot, but she's NICE. Anyway, it would probably take three days with her for me to finally get what she's talking about when she says "Fibonacci."

Day 1
This is all too confusing.

Day 2
Lemme concentrate — I know I can figure it out.

Day 3
Aha! I get it now!

I've never been with a teacher for that long, and I've never gone on a field trip where you sleep there. That's another new thing about middle school, I guess. I wonder what the beds will be like... and the food. Will I have to take showers with everyone else? Will kids make fun of my pajamas? What am I getting myself into? I made a quiz about that once, how what you wear to sleep reveals your personality whether you want it to or not.

THE PAJAMA GAME

Pick out the sleepwear you like best. Choose some slippers and a bathrobe to go with it. The combination you pick says a lot about who you are!

Ⓐ furry, zip-up pajamas

Ⓑ your clothes (why bother to change?)

Ⓒ oversized T-shirt

Ⓓ top and boxers

If you chose mostly A's, you like to be warm and toasty.

If you chose mostly B's, you like things to be easy and convenient.

If you chose mostly C's, you don't get cold easily.

If you chose mostly D's, you wear whatever your mom buys you.

If you chose a mix of all the letters, you have a very distinctive style!

And if you're getting sleepy reading about pajamas, then it's time to go to bed.

I wonder what kind of pajamas I should pack. Maybe I should get some new ones just for the trip. I'll ask Carly what she's bringing, and that's what I'll do.

Carly's really excited about this field trip. She says it's going to be great.

Who cares what kind of PJ's you wear?

You can always borrow some of mine.

Just think, Amelia, we'll be together all the time. We won't be bugged by my brothers.

And you'll get a break from Cleo. Imagine — three days without your sister!

We could sleep on the floor for that kind of trip — the beds don't matter!

I hadn't even thought of that part! It'll be like a vacation from home! No rude noises from Cleo, no more smelling that nasty stuff she uses to strip the hair off her legs, and no more listening to her terrible singing (screeching, I should say). And it'll be a break from Mom, too. No nagging to clean my room, floss my teeth, or do my homework, and if I don't want to eat rubbery green beans, I won't have to. Teachers care about homework, not vegetables left on your plate.

I was really getting excited about the class trip...
up until tonight at dinner, when something happened
that changed EVERYTHING! Horrible, horrible
news — my life in middle school is doomed,
DOOMED!

Cleo said the WORST thing that could have
possibly come out of her mouth.

I almost choked on my macaroni! Cleo working with my class? That's my worst nightmare! She's EXACTLY what I want to avoid on this trip! It's a collision of worlds!

school world ↓   home world ↓

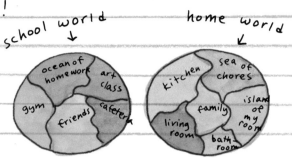

school world: ocean of homework, art class, gym, friends, cafeteria

home world: sea of chores, kitchen, island of my room, family, living room, bath-room

The only worse-case scenario I can imagine is if Mom became one of my teachers — that would be a supernova!

I can just see Mom saying the WORST things in front of everybody! ↓

And Mom seemed to think it was great — as if I want Cleo with me. Doesn't she understand what a DISASTER this is? Way worse than a 10.2 earthquake or hurricane force winds!

Amelia, did you brush your teeth this morning?

You're not wearing the panties with the holes, are you?

I'm not sure which would be more embarrassing — hearing Mom say "panties" or everyone knowing about my holey underwear.

Isn't that nice, Amelia? You'll have your sister with you.

She can watch out for you and make sure you're okay.

Mom gets more clueless the older she gets. When has Cleo EVER taken care of me? And why would I need her to anyway? I can take care of MYSELF! And if I couldn't, Cleo is the LAST person on earth I'd want to depend on!

Cleo was so happy with what Mom said, she practically purred. She KNOWS I don't want her around, and she's GLOATING!

Of course I can, Amelia, and all that sisterly togetherness will be wonderful. PURRRR!

I WANTED TO PUKE!!

Mom and Cleo both looked at me, waiting for me to say something. Only there was nothing to say, not to them. I just mumbled that I had a stomachache and asked to be excused from the table. Once I was safe in my room, I did the only thing I could think of —

I called Carly in a panic.

What am I going to do? I'll get the flu! I'll have to stay home! ANYTHING but going with Cleo! She'll ruin my life— I KNOW she will!

Calm down, Amelia. Don't you think you're overreacting? So what if Cleo goes too? She's an aide. She won't be in charge of you.

Yeah, but before I had to worry about a teacher hating me because he'd taught Cleo and assumed I was like her, a mean trickster. NOW I have to worry about the kids in my class meeting my gross, rude sister and assuming I have the same disgusting habits. It's a NIGHTMARE!

Maybe that won't happen. I've met Cleo, and I don't think you're at all like her just because you're sisters.

You don't know Cleo like I do. She's HORRIBLE! She'll do SOMETHING to embarrass me — she can't help it, it's part of her genetic code!

Carly didn't get it. How could she? Her brothers are normal—not creatures from the black lagoon, like Cleo. It's bad enough I have to live with her. Does everyone have to know we're related?

I wrote to Nadia. Even though she's an only child, she'll understand. She knows what a disaster Cleo is. ⟍

Dear Nadia,
  Here I am in middle school, where suddenly your reputation really matters, and I have to deal with Cleo contagion. Normally we only see each other before and after school, but NOW she's a student helper on our class science trip, so we'll be together *all the time*! How can I survive unscathed? It will be the most embarrassing field trip of my life!

yours till the mouse traps,
amelia
HELP!

HAVE A SEAT
23¢

Nadia Kurz
61 South St.
Barton, CA
91010

It'll be like kindergarten all over again, only instead of having girl cooties, I'll have Cleo cooties.

Ay, ay, ay...

Marshmallow pie, ay, ay...

Spit in my eye, eye, eye...

← bad, off-key singing—head for the hills, quick

I tried to tell Ms. Reilly that I might have to miss the field trip, but my brain didn't work fast enough to think up a convincing excuse.

Lying to teachers is like lying to parents — you can't let them smell your fear! If you believe your lie, then they'll believe it, but if a hint of doubt creeps into your voice, the game's up and you've lost.

Um, Ms. Reilly, I'm afraid I'll have to miss the class trip. I'm really sorry.

Miss the trip? Of course you won't! Unless you're in the hospital— and you look fine to me.

It's just that, um, my dad will be visiting from out of town and I don't want to miss him.

And I'm sure your dad wouldn't want you to miss the trip. How about I call him up for a little chat?

NO! I mean, no, that's okay, I'll ask him myself.

You do that then. And if he says you can't go, I'll ring him up and we can discuss it.

SIGH!

What a disaster! There's no escaping Cleo! I had the worst headache ever today.

Carly's still trying to convince me everything will be fine. Mom insists it will all be wonderful. And Cleo, even Cleo, suddenly seems to imagine we're a different kind of sisters than we really are, like she's been watching too many sappy movies about sisterly love.

Amelia, I'm really looking forward to this. It's going to be so much fun!

Just think, we'll have some great sister-bonding time! Like a long sleep-over party!

This isn't the real Cleo. She's been replaced by → an alien clone.

← Only something extreme, like a personality transplant, would make Cleo really like this.

And we've never had a trip together, just the two of us, away from Mom or Dad.

Of course, Cleo's probably saying this to impress Mom. I know she's trying to convince Mom to let her take the bus into the city, and she's going out of her way to show how responsible she is — like emptying the dishwasher <u>before</u> Mom asks her, taking out the garbage when it's not even her turn, and now acting like a sweet big sister when she's NOT!

But no one asks me what I think, what I want — and what I DON'T want. Top of that list is "bonding" with Cleo. I don't want to be in the same room as her, much less get close to her! And she's never wanted to be friends with me, either. What's all this lovey-dovey, nicey-nice stuff about? It's got to be a trick, a way to get on Mom's good side, and NO WAY am I going to help Cleo with that! But I have to be careful what I say in front of Mom, or I'll look like the mean, bad sister, when really that's Cleo.

How can I beg to stay home now? HOW CAN I GET OUT OF THIS?

I'M DOOMED!

Tonight at dinner I felt like a prisoner having her last meal before being led to execution. Tomorrow we leave for the class trip. I still haven't heard from Nadia, and it looks like there's no escape.

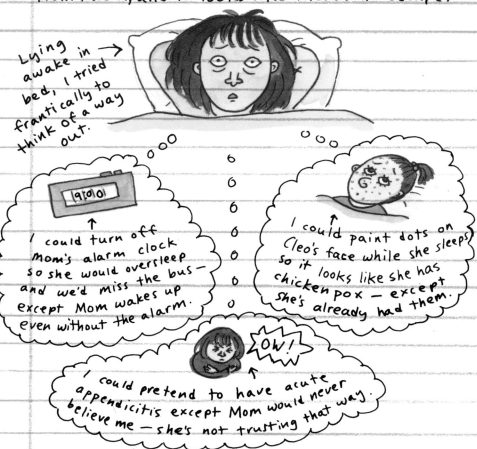

Lying in awake in bed, I tried frantically to think of a way out.

I could turn off mom's alarm clock so she would oversleep and we'd miss the bus — except Mom wakes up even without the alarm.

I could paint dots on Cleo's face while she sleeps so it looks like she has chicken pox — except she's already had them.

OW!

I could pretend to have acute appendicitis except Mom would never believe me — she's not trusting that way.

I was trapped. Only a miracle could save me, like a sudden mudslide blocking the road to the science camp or all the teachers going on strike.

I wanted desperately to stop time, but morning came anyway. Even though I deliberately left my backpack in the house so we'd have to come back and get it and miss the bus, Mom noticed I didn't have it with me and made me put in on and marched me to the car. There really was no escape.

At least Carly was happy to see me.

Amelia, over here! Let's make sure we sit together on the bus.

I admit I was glad to have someone waiting for me. Especially since Cleo didn't. I mean, it's my class, my friends. Except that meant without her own friends to join, Cleo stuck to me — like glue.

Cleo's glue-all — for instant bonding or sticky messes

On the bus I got to sit next to Carly — good. But then Cleo  got on and sat next to me — bad. Luckily Carly had brought her MP3 player and extra headphones so we could listen to music and not Cleo — good. Unluckily Cleo got carsick like she always does — bad, VERY bad! And the window on the bus wouldn't open — WORST OF ALL!

This is going to be a very long class trip.

And the teachers didn't make things better. Ms. Reilly and Mr. Wu, the other science teacher, took turns leading us in stupid games like science trivia. Like who invented penicillin and what is it anyway? Cleo naturally didn't answer a single question — she was too busy with her barf bag. And Carly and I were concentrating so hard on NOT breathing, we didn't get any right either. It's hard to think when you're trying NOT to smell, taste, see, or hear what's right next to you.

LET US OUTTA HERE! HELP!!

At last we got to the ranger station at Drake's Beach. Carly and I practically threw ourselves out of the bus. We gulped in fresh air like we'd been drowning (drowning in Cleo fumes, that is). I never knew how good salty ocean air could taste!

Cleo looked so pale and exhausted, I almost felt sorry for her. →

Almost.

Cleo was so weak, she couldn't even carry in her duffel bag so I had to do it. Hah! Here she was supposed to be looking after me, and I ended up taking care of her! Shows what Mom knows! I was right — there's no good part to having Cleo here. It's bad, bad, all BAD. Bad beginning (a vomitrocious one!), bad middle, and bound to end badly (there's always the barfy bus ride back).

After we put our stuff away in the dorms, we were divided into groups and met our teachers. Even though Ms. Reilly and Mr. Wu came with us, they won't lead the classes. Instead they'll work with the instructors here.

Ranger Station
Guides and
Teachers

Mr. Welkin has a warm, friendly face. He looks like someone who spends a lot of time outdoors.

Ms. Cook is young and enthusiastic. She just started teaching but seems like she knows a lot of stuff.

Ms. Reilly (and the other teacher from our school, Mr. Wu) will go from group to group.

She'll spend half her time with Mr. Welkin and his students and half with Ms. Cook and those kids.

> We have a lot to cover in three days, so you need to really listen! You'll learn about the tidal zone and the fascinating forms of life that thrive in this unique environment.

I just hope I thrive, not wither away, sharing my environment with Cleo. Maybe she had to come on the trip, maybe I have to sleep in the same dorm as her, but I could still pray she wouldn't be assigned to my group. She could help the other 6th graders and leave me alone.

But before the 8th-grade aides were assigned, we had to find out which group we'd be in, Mr. Welkin's or Ms. Cook's.

GOOD NEWS!

Carly and I were put in the same group! We're both with Mr. Welkin. I was so busy worrying about Cleo, I forgot to think about the possibility that Carly and I could be separated. We're lucky that didn't happen. Then we waited to hear which 8th grader would help our group. I kept chanting in my head:

Not Cleo, not Cleo, not Cleo, not Cleo, not Cleo, not Cleo, not Cleo, not Cleo, not Cleo...

Please not Cleo, not Cleo, not Cleo, not Cleo, not Cleo, not Cleo...

And with Mr. Welkin's group, Cleo.

I felt like a balloon with all the air gone out of it.

My WORST fear had come true!

I guess the fresh air made Cleo feel better because just when I felt awful, she looked completely recovered.

Yeah, I wanted to buy a lottery ticket, I was oozing so much good fortune.

Funny, when I first started going to the same school as Cleo, she pretended she didn't even know me. Now that she's conveniently far away from her friends, she's all buddy-buddy. She's NEVER called me "Sis" before.

So why start now? Maybe she's trying to impress the teachers, especially after being NO HELP at all on the bus (just a source of toxic pollution). Maybe she's trying to prove she CAN take care of me after I had to lug her duffel bag for her. Whatever it is, I don't buy it.

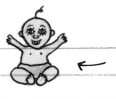

She can't suddenly call me "Sis" and have me believe we're all lovey-dovey. Times have changed. She hasn't loved me since I was a baby and she called me "Pumpkin."

Then I grew into a toddler and started grabbing all her toys, and she called me "Brat" and "Pig-O."

Then I started school and learned to read and had my own friends, and she called me "Dummy" and "Booger."

Now I'm "Sis"? I don't think so!

No matter what <u>she</u> calls <u>me</u>, no way am I calling <u>her</u> "Sis." I do have a lot of other names for her, though.

Mostly I call her "Jelly Roll Nose" — she hates it.

Sometimes I call her "Crumb Volcano" because of the way she spews when she eats — GROSS!!

When she's really mad, I call her "Snort Face" because of the delicate way she expresses anger.

AMELIA!

I have only one choice for survival — I'm NOT going to be "Sis." I'll have to pretend Cleo is invisible. (That or I'll have to be invisible.)

That means enough writing about Cleo. It's time to think about this place, Marina Headlands. It's like a nature center, only with classrooms, dorms, and a cafeteria. Each day we'll do some science, some arts and crafts, and a nature hike. But the biggest challenge (besides the slimy showers and smelly toilets) is the climbing wall.

side view of climbing wall ←

Using the bumps on the wall as handholds and footholds, everyone tries to climb as far as they can. You're supposed to make it all the way to the top, but so far no one has. Well, it's only the first day; I'm sure we'll get better. →

Usually I'm the worst in the class in sports because I'm so short and small, but I actually made it up the wall farther than anyone else. Finally, an advantage to having less body weighing me down! Carly did pretty good too. Cleo was predictably pathetic. She never does ANY sports. ←

Unfortunately Cleo isn't cooperating with my invisible plan. She's all TOO obvious. There's no way to avoid her from the beginning of the day to the end.

the hike

morning

Cleo bellowing at the top of her lungs (believe me, that's LOUD!)

HUP two, three, FOUR!

March, march, MARCH!

noon

making sun prints

Um, your shadow blocks out the sun.

night

campfire talk

Wow! Is that the Big Shovel?

Carly kept whispering all day.

Just ignore her.

I'm trying, REALLY trying!

Then we had to get ready for bed, and I remembered all the things I had worried about <u>before</u> I knew Cleo was coming — real worries like getting undressed before everybody and having the right pajamas and sleeping in a strange bed and hearing scary noises at night.

Good thing I had Carly with me. She let me borrow a pair of her pajamas, so I wouldn't look dorky. (Carly's automatically cool. I don't know how she does it, but she is.) I changed as quickly as I could without looking at anyone else changing (that old magical trick of thinking if you can't see someone, they can't see you). Then I got into bed and since I was safely covered, tried to see what everyone else was doing without looking like I was looking.

It was a fascinating study in itself.

Lucinda put some green goop on her face and went to sleep like that.

Jessica brushed her hair 100 times — she actually counted out loud to be sure.

Sharleen brought 6 pairs of pajamas for 3 nights and spent 20 minutes deciding which ones to wear.

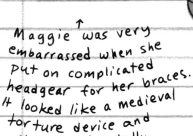

↑
Maggie was very embarrassed when she put on complicated headgear for her braces. It looked like a medieval torture device and <u>she</u> looked totally tormented.

↑
Sue wasn't at all embarrassed about clipping her toenails — GROSS!

↑
Charisse, who's so perfect about everything, wore slippers that matched her nightgown and had a cute little light to clip onto her book so she could read.

And Cleo? →

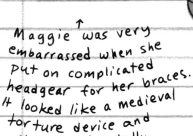

← I already knew about Cleo's bedtime habits and now everyone else would too.

↑
First she popped her pimples, then she rubbed some evil-smelling goo on her face, then she changed into boxer shorts with hearts on them and a bright pink T-shirt that said "BIG MAMA" on it, then she bellowed "Sweet dreams, everybody," waking up a couple of kids who had already fallen asleep, then she did what she always does, every night for as long as I've known her.

She snored.

It's been a long time since Cleo and I shared a room.
I forgot how loud she could be. Carly and I hardly slept at all.

How long will this go on?

I hate to tell you — the whole night.

Charisse, of course, had earplugs.

I was tempted to grab them out of her ears and put them in my own.

At 7 a.m. sharp the Cleo alarm went off, and it was time to start the day again. I don't know how I'll survive this week.

Everyone was groggy and exhausted at breakfast from sleeping so badly. Except for Cleo. And Charisse. Before we had a chance to really wake up, Ms. Reilly came to our table, eager not to waste one precious educational minute.

I was hoping we could start with a nice, easy art project. Eight in the morning is too early to face science and all of Ms. Reilly's facts. By 9 a.m. we were at the tide pools, which would have been fine if we could have just wandered around and looked at different sea life, but we had an assignment. "Serious work to do" according to Ms. Reilly.

I used to think science was a lot of fun, but today I learned a science secret — it's 50% fun and 50% booooooooooooring. The good part was the hike along the tide pools. At least I thought it was fun. Sharleen complained about getting sand on her shoes. I could understand if it was getting in her shoes, but on her shoes?

Then came the boring part. And even more sand — on our hands this time. Sharleen looked REALLY grossed out. Maybe it wasn't because of sand. Maybe it was because we had to collect snails. Not regular snails, sea snails. Our group found a lot of humor in that, due to the shell's resemblance to a certain someone's nose.

Hey, Cleo, your nose is running —

— away from me!

Wow, noses are everywhere!

I'll sniff one out!

Cleo was NOT amused. →

Mama!

At first I thought the nose jokes were funny, but then they got to be too much, even for me.

Hey, Amelia, what's it like to live with Cleo? Do you have to shield yourself with an umbrella every time she sneezes?

I bet you can't hide any secrets from her. She's sure to sniff them out.

Is Cleo giving you special privileges since you're sisters — like letting you nose out the rest of us?

Hey, Cleo's helped me find lots of snails — she really has a nose for it.

Not that I felt sorry for Cleo — I felt sorry for me. I wished I didn't have a sister. I wished she would be buried by a sand dune or swallowed by a wave.

But she wasn't. And instead of trying to be less obvious, the way I would be if people made fun of me, she started making her own jokes.

Listen, if you had a nose like mine, you might be sensitive too. After all, my nose can smell the jam between my toes without me bending over.

My nose is so big, the airlines charge me excess baggage for it. It's so big, I can stand in one time zone and blow my nose in the other.

My nose is so big that when I snore, not only do I feel the bed shake, everyone else in the room does too! My nose is so big that when I stand sideways, it looks like a nose wearing a face and not the other way around.

I guess she thought everyone was laughing with her then, not at her. I'm not so sure. I just wanted to sink into the sand and disappear. Who wants a sister who's a clown? Or I should say, who wants a sister who's a walking, talking, snorting, snoring nose?

The thing about the ocean is, it's hard to stay mad or worried or even embarrassed near it. The air smells so good and the sound of the surf is so calming that you can't help but relax and have fun. Even Cleo couldn't ruin things. And I have to give her credit — she can have good ideas sometimes. After we had all found enough snails, she asked Mr. Welkin if we could play in the sandy part of the beach for a little while. He said yes, so we took off our shoes, rolled up our pants, and played tag with the waves. Cleo even did cartwheels! That got rid of the bad taste of all the nose jokes. Everyone just had a lot of fun. I guess that was the bonding Ms. Reilly was talking about.

Except Sharleen, the girl with all the pajamas, wouldn't take her shoes off. Tyler said it was because she was afraid of water. Corey teased her for being a coward. Lucinda accused her of being too stuck-up to play with the rest of us. Suddenly all the focus was _off_ Cleo and _on_ Sharleen. I felt bad for her. Maybe Sharleen just doesn't like the feel of wet sand on her toes. After all, she doesn't like it on her _shoes_. If she's fussy enough to need so many pajamas, that could be her problem.

When everyone put their shoes back on and we started walking back to the classroom with our pails full of snails, kids kept on teasing Sharleen until Mr. Welkin told them to quit it.

Are you in love with your shoes soooo much you can't bear to take them off?

Hey, do you wear those shoes to bed? I _never_ see you take them off!

Are they glued on or something?

Sharleen looked straight ahead. I could see she was trying hard to ignore it all, but that's hard to do. →

Why didn't she just take off her shoes? Then everyone would leave her alone. The worst crime a kid can commit in middle school is to stick out. Even I know that!

I guess I should be grateful she took the attention away from me and Cleo. Seems like some kids, especially Tyler and Corey, need someone to pick on at all times. As long as it's not me, I should relax, but I can't.

Carly and I looked at each other. We were both thinking the same thing.

"Hey, Sharleen," Carly said, "slow down. We can't keep up with you." Sharleen looked surprised but she waited for us to catch up.

"Sorry about the shoe business," I said.

She shrugged. "It's ok. I don't care."

"The same way I don't care that my sister is the teacher's aide?" I asked.

She smiled and looked me in the face. "Yeah. Exactly. That kind of not caring." I rolled my eyes. "You know," she said, "she's really not so bad. It just seems that way to you because you're her sister."

Maybe. I'm not sure. But for a while at least, it didn't matter. I didn't think about Cleo at all. It was a great hike back. We talked about all kinds of things, Carly, Sharleen, and I. I think I've made my first new friend in middle school.

maybe Sharleen's shoes give her confidence or maybe she's just got cold feet. It doesn't matter to me.

So that was all good. What came next wasn't. We went back to the classroom, each with a bucket of at least 5O snails, and we had to measure the opening in ALL of them. ALL FIFTY!! The point was to chart variations in growth in the snail population, but the whole time I was measuring, all I could think was WHY? What difference does it make? Was this one of those useless bits of information grown-ups insist you learn for no obvious reason?

STUFF YOU HAVE TO LEARN BUT WILL <u>NEVER</u> <u>EVER</u> USE

↓

↑
the names of capitals—
all the state capitals does
after high school this?
ANYONE ask you this?
Isn't this kind of information
what an atlas is for?

↑
negative numbers—
they seem so crabby
and mean (all that
negativity), so why
bother with them?
Seems better to stay
far away from their
bad moods.

↑
cursive
handwriting—
come on, this
is the computer
generation.
Who writes
by hand
anymore
(except me in
my notebook and
I PRINT!)?

↑
how to find the area
of a circle or a square—
or of any shape—the only
area you really need to
know is your area code.

I'm really stellus magnificus!

↑
measurements—
does it matter if
there are 2 cups
in a pint? When do
you measure a pint
anyway? And who
cares if there are 3
feet in a yard when
most of the world uses
the metric system?

↑
the scientific names
for things — who
calls a starfish
anything but a
starfish? Do you call
a dog a canine?
(Wait, that's a tooth,
isn't it?)

The first 10 snails were fine. The next 10 were bearable. By the 10 after that, I had to blink a lot to get my eyes to focus. I was seeing snails everywhere — not just double, but triple and quadruple.

← a blurry haze of snail shells →

There wasn't even a break at dinner. Ms. Reilly read us some of the other class's measurements while we tried to eat the dried-out meatloaf and gluey mashed potatoes. Talk about a way to ruin your appetite! Bad food + boring lists of numbers = a bad stomachache. At least the droning kept everyone's attention off Cleo and her bad table manners. Does she have to shovel so much food at once? Does she have to burp so loudly? Does she have to smack her lips? For once I wanted to hear every detail of Ms. Reilly's nonstop talking, even if it was about slimy snails. Anything was better than the sounds of Cleo eating!

Sharleen could see how annoyed I was. "Your sister's not so bad," she whispered in my ear. "You should see my brother — he's a master of chewing with his mouth open!"

Just then Cleo laughed so hard at something Lucinda said, milk shot out of her nose! That's WAY worse than openmouthed chomping. I wanted to crawl under the table.

why does it matter to me so much when she's the one who's gross?

After all, I didn't snort cow juice. I eat and drink politely. It's not fair that stuff I can't control reflects on me.

dripping milk from Cleo explosion

The ~~wierd~~ ~~weird~~ ~~wierd~~ weird thing is, Cleo didn't seem at all

AAAGH! I'll graduate college and still spell this word wrong!

embarrassed. She just wiped her face and laughed at herself along with everyone else. Either she's being really smart or really stupid. I can't tell which.

"You still think your brother is worse?" I asked Sharleen.

She shrugged. "I can't help it — I admire Cleo's guts. Nothing seems to embarrass her."

"Exactly!" I said. "That's the problem!"

Maybe I'm just too sensitive. I admit that everything Cleo does seems louder and more embarrassing to me because she's my sister. I can't help it. Last night I dreamed of snails and Cleo all mixed together. It was a horrible combination.

HELP!

Measure me! I bet you can't measure up to me!

Cleo was a giant, and she kept yelling at me to measure her nose. I was afraid of falling into the black hole of her nostril, but I measured the opening just as she...

...sneezed!

I went flying in a cloud of snot, and right before I splatted on the ground, I woke up.

My teeth were chattering, I was so terrified. It took a long time before I could calm down enough to fall asleep again. The roar of Cleo's snores did NOT help. I didn't need to be reminded of the proximity of her nose.

I looked around the dorm room. It was so dark, everyone looked like mounds on their cots. I couldn't tell Sharleen from Carly, Lucinda from Charisse. The only person who was more than a lump of blankets was Cleo. She was a noise machine, the source of a growling

GNAKKAKKAGG.

It was like she was a giant nose, just like in my dream. I tried counting snores since I couldn't ignore them until my eyelids got heavy, and I must have fallen asleep because I had another dream. Cleo's nose was in it again, and it was even SCARIER!

In the dream I was in science camp, and Cleo was in charge of my group.

Only it wasn't really Cleo — it was her nose, a GIANT Cleo nose with legs and arms.

When the smoke from the sneeze cleared, Cleo had disappeared. Where did she go, I wondered. Then my nose started to twitch, to itch, to snort. I knew that snort! It could only come from Cleo's jelly roll nose! AND IT WAS ON MY FACE!!!

All the other kids started laughing and pointing at me. I pulled desperately at the nose, but it wouldn't come off. It just kept making farting noises. Even Carly was doubled over. Sharleen, too.

It was worse than the nightmares I used to have of going to school in my underwear! Everyone was laughing at me. And the nose <u>wouldn't</u> come off! When I woke up, I felt my face in a panic, sure my dream had come true. But there was my normal nose, right where it belonged. I was <u>so</u> relieved, I felt I could face anything because at least I <u>wasn't</u> Cleo.   ← all the possible noses I could have →

Brushing my teeth that morning, lined up at the sinks with the other girls, it occurred to me that school is a lesson on how to handle embarrassing moments as much as how to solve math equations or understand history. Like public showers. So far <u>no one</u> has used them here. Washing your face is one thing, undressing in front of everyone is something else. Maybe that's why Sharleen keeps her shoes on — this class trip is about more than bonding, it's about seeing parts of other students you really don't want to see. And I don't mean just parts of people's bodies. I mean private secrets that are hard to keep private when you sleep, eat, and spend all day together.

SECRETS OF
CLASS 6A

ABSOLUTELY
PRIVATE

NO UNAUTHORIZED PEEKING
ALLOWED

FOR AMELIA'S EYES
ONLY

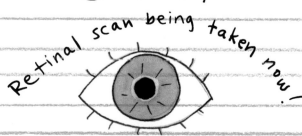

Retinal scan being taken now!

MY COLLECTION OF LITTLE-KNOWN FACTS PEOPLE WOULD PREFER TO KEEP UNDERWOOD

MY COLLECTION OF LITTLE-KNOWN FACTS PEOPLE WOULD PREFER TO KEEP <u>UN</u>KNOWN

↓

Carly sleeps with a retainer.

Kim has athlete's foot (<u>not</u> an athletic foot!).

Olivia hums when she brushes her teeth.

Monday

Lucinda wears underwear with days of the week written on them so she remembers to change them.

Maya actually likes the grandma-ish nightgown her mom makes her wear.

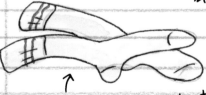

Carmen wears her brother's hand-me-down socks.

Vanessa keeps worry dolls under her pillow to keep away bad dreams (I need these!).

I WONDER WHAT KINDS OF SECRETS THE BOYS HAVE — I CAN ONLY IMAGINE.

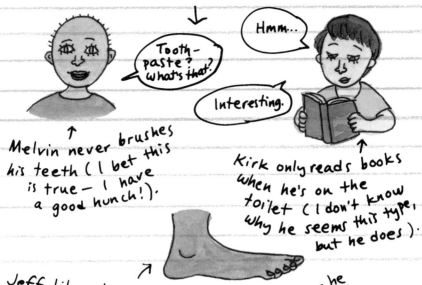

Melvin never brushes his teeth (I bet this is true — I have a good hunch!).

Kirk only reads books when he's on the toilet (I don't know why he seems this type, but he does).

Jeff likes to paint his toenails blue — he borrows polish from his sister.

Sam practices his "looks" in front of a mirror — he's certainly polished enough.

Clark is Cleo's match in snoring — the way their names start the same is a clue.

← coyote

I guess we all have something to be embarrassed about — and my something is Cleo. At breakfast I sat as far away from her as possible. I thought kids would tease me about her. Instead they said nice things!

"We're lucky we got Cleo for our student aide," Corey said.

↑
black
bear

"Yeah," Lucinda agreed. "The other class got Kendall, and he's really bossy."

mountain
lion
↓

"I heard he made Carlos measure all 50 of his snail shells <u>twice</u> because he was talking!"

"That's so unfair!" Maya said. "You can talk and measure at the same time."

"Cleo can talk and do <u>anything</u> at the same time," Sharleen said. "And she's funny, too!"

skunk
↓

↑
elk

Could they really be talking about my sister?

After breakfast we went on a nature hike, looking for animal prints and scat (that's a nice, clean scientific word for poop). We found some raccoon prints by a stream but not much else.

↑
deer

deer
mouse →

← squirrel

↑
raccoon

It was turning into a dud of a hike. Then Sharleen wanted to rest —something about getting the sand out of her shoes (that girl and shoes!). Everyone groaned. Maya said Sharleen was holding the group back. Tyler said we should go on without her. But Cleo thought a break was a great idea. She plopped herself down on a boulder next to Sharleen.

"We've walked enough for a while," Cleo said. "Now we can wait for the animals to come to us instead of us looking for them."

I rolled my eyes at Carly. Yeah, right, we could just sit there and see nature if grass and trees were all you cared about.

Then suddenly Cleo stood up, pointing with one hand and waving with the other. I knew something was up when she did this SILENTLY. We all looked where she was pointing, and there stood the biggest deer I've ever seen.

Because it wasn't a deer — it was an elk! And behind it were more elk, a whole herd of elk. →

We all held our breath, it was so magical. I couldn't ← move. I just stared. Finally the herd melted into the forest. Gone.

It was the best part of the whole hike, and it was because of Sharleen and her sensitive feet. Maya walked next to her on the way back like she was her new best friend. Tyler said it was a good thing Sharleen was with us or we would have really missed out. I thought Cleo would want to take some credit for seeing the elk, but she didn't.

When we got back, I thought we'd have to chart the snail shell measurements we made yesterday, but Mr. Welkin didn't think we'd had enough activity.

Now that we've warmed up our muscles, it's time for a real challenge. By the end of the week I expect you all to make it to the top.

Let's see how many of you can do it now.

Most kids weren't exactly jumping ↓ with enthusiasm.

I used up my legs already.

Don't we get a snack first?

How about tomorrow?

I wanted to be the first to make it all the way, or at least the first girl. What I like about climbing is that a lot of it is mental, figuring out where to put your hand or foot next. The most important thing isn't whether you're strong or fast but whether heights make you nervous or not. Rule #1 is Never Look Down.

Naturally Cleo, the Carsick Queen, started sweating and shaking when she was only a yard off the ground. Sharleen tried to encourage her.

Everyone else started cheering her on too (except me).

C'mon, Cleo, you can do it! Lead the way!

Go, Cleo!

Cleo power!

She almost got to the top. Almost. A couple of feet from it, Cleo stopped, just clinging to the handholds and footholds. The kids yelled even louder, but she was frozen. She shook her head and started back down.

The chanting stopped and a huge groan or sigh swept through the crowd. Then it was quiet. Too quiet. When Cleo stepped back on the ground, she looked like she was going to cry, but suddenly someone yelled one last "Cleo!" Kids cheered and the boy nearest her clapped her on the back. Another kid high-fived her. Cleo smiled and shook her head.

"Next time," she promised. "Next time for sure I'll make it to the top."

I have to admit I was impressed with Cleo. She started cheering for the next kid to try, Sharleen.

And there was no more grumbling about being too tired or wanting a snack. Now everyone wanted to climb!

When it was my turn, I could hear Cleo yelling my name loudest of all. I was tempted to look at her, but I remembered rule #1 - NEVER LOOK DOWN! So I looked up and pictured everyone's voices as a big hand shoving me forward.

AND I MADE IT! I DID IT! ALL THE WAY TO THE TOP!!

Then I did look down. Cleo was smiling and waving and Carly was jumping up and down, all excited for me. For a minute I was so happy, I didn't even feel dizzy. It was funny - I felt like I'd climbed to the top for myself and for Cleo.

YAY!! AMELIAAA!!!

Then I had to blink my eyes so the ground would stop moving. I focused on my hands in front of me, took a deep breath, and remembered what Mr. Welkin had said - I had to let go of the wall and rappel down.

Only my hands didn't want to let go of the wall and grab onto the rope. I was so high up, it was hard to trust the slender, swaying rope.

AMELIA AMELIA AMELIA

Carly had done it. Sharleen, Lucinda, Tyler, Max, and Omar had done it. Lots of kids had done it. I took another deep breath —
          and   I let go of the wall.

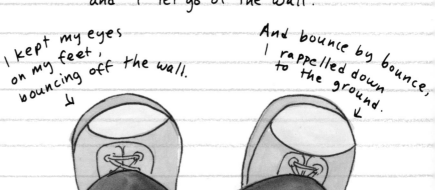

I kept my eyes on my feet, bouncing off the wall. ↓

And bounce by bounce, I rappelled down to the ground. ↙

IT WAS GREAT!!! I felt like I was flying! When my feet landed, it was like I'd taken a _much_ longer journey than 20 feet up a wall!

Carly ran up and hugged me. Cleo helped me out of the harness and said I was Supergirl. Sharleen said she knew I could do it. I knew that too. Today may have started with a nightmare, but it had turned into a fantastic, amazing, wonderful, incredible day!

That night when we were all in bed, Cleo broke the "no talking after 9 p.m. rule" (and she's the person in charge of _enforcing_ the rules).

"Well," she began, "I think that was my most embarrassing moment for the year — not making it even _close_ to the top of the climbing wall."

"More embarrassing than getting carsick on the bus ride?" asked Olivia.

"More embarrassing than blowing milk out your nose?," asked Lucinda.

"Definitely!" said Cleo. "I'm used to that other stuff."

There was a long moment where no one talked. Then Cleo asked, "So what's your most embarrassing moment? Here's your chance to get it out of your system. This is like truth _and_ dare — do you dare to tell the truth?"

The darkness was so thick, it made the quiet seem even louder.

More silence.

"Come on," Cleo urged. "It won't be so embarrassing once you describe it."

Part of me wanted Cleo to SHUT UP! What if she told an embarrassing story about me? Like the time I fell into the fountain or the time I followed a complete stranger around the grocery store thinking she was Mom (I was really little and grown-ups look similar from the knees down). Or the time I tried to hatch an egg from the refrigerator. I'd have no choice — I'd have to cover her face with my pillow. Even if she didn't spill the beans about the time I wore my shirt backwards for the whole day, I HATED that she knew all this stuff about me.

Besides all that, I couldn't stand her being all buddy-buddy with my friends. They can't like her AND me.

But part of me, the not-sister part, wanted Cleo to keep on talking. It would be fun in the dark to hear about the embarrassing stuff you could never talk about in the light of day. I didn't want to admit anything, and I sure didn't want Cleo to tell any incriminating stories, but I hoped someone would confess.

Then a voice said, "Okay, I'll start." It was Carly! "Here's my most embarrassing moment. I was in 3rd grade and playing tetherball during recess. I had on a new skirt I really loved. I loved it so much, I wore it even though it was a little big on me. I swung real hard at the tetherball — AND MY SKIRT FELL DOWN! I pulled it back up so fast, I don't think anyone even noticed, but I sure did! And I kept staring at everyone all day, trying to figure out if they'd seen my underwear or not."

← underwear!

legs! →

← completely visible!

Everybody laughed. That broke the ice. Suddenly everyone had a funny embarrassing story to tell. I stopped worrying about Cleo and just listened and laughed with everyone else. It was amazing that not one of the stories made me cringe with shared embarrassment. They were all just hilarious.

Embarrassing
Great and

The funny thing was, what really embarrassed one person didn't bother the rest of us at all. You think everyone's laughing at you, but no one thinks about it as much as you do. Like years later, Carly still blushed thinking about her skirt falling down, but no one else even remembered it.

getting a bean stuck up your nose and having to go to the doctor to remove it

tracking dog poop into your best friend's house

not watching where you're going and walking into a post — the physical pain is NOTHING next to the embarrassment

burping loudly during silent reading

thinking it's Pajama Day at school when it's really the NEXT day

Everyone had a story to tell.

"I stood up to give an oral report — and farted!"

"The teacher said my name wrong in front of the whole class. Instead of calling me Peggy, she called me Piggy!"

"I didn't mean to, but I sneezed in the teacher's face!"

"No one told me I had something between my front teeth, and it was school photo day. I tore up all my pictures but I couldn't change the class photo!"

I was laughing hard with everyone else until Maya noticed I hadn't said anything yet.

"Come on, Amelia," she said. "It's your turn."

I couldn't admit my MOST embarrassing moment because it's way longer than a moment — it's my whole life! It's having Cleo for my sister! But everyone in my class loves her now, so how can I say that? I couldn't. I didn't. But I had to say SOMETHING or I was about to suffer another embarrassing moment.

So I told about the time I went to a pool party, only instead of packing my good bathing suit, Mom gave me the ugly old lady one WITH A SKIRT!

I tried not to wear it, but somebody opened my bag and found it and then I _had_ to put it on.

I didn't know they still made suits like that!

I didn't know they EVER made them for kids. I've only seen them on old ladies.

I've always hated that memory, but after I told the story, I laughed as much as the other kids. I guess we really are bonding on this trip, if that's what it means to know embarrassing secrets about people. Only they're not secrets anymore — or embarrassing. Now, they're just funny stories. At breakfast everyone was in a great mood, like they'd gotten rid of a heavy weight last night. Everyone except me.

Watching Cleo laugh and joke with the kids at the table, I had an amazing thought. →

If Cleo wasn't my sister, would I like her? Would I think she was funny like everyone else did?

↑
Why should she be embarrassed after all? She was just having a good time.

Maybe the embarrassing stuff was part of me, not part of her. After all, I didn't have to wear Cleo like an ugly bathing suit. I didn't even have to sit next to her. I wasn't sure what to think anymore. It was easier to measure snails than figure this out.

Today we charted our snail shell measurements so we could see the variations in the snail population. Having it laid out in a graph like that was pretty cool. You could see how there was a big difference from one end of the scale to the other. Kind of like with people. I could make a _lot_ of interesting charts showing that range.

VARIATIONS IN HUMAN POPULATION

← You could graph all kinds of things, →
from the physical —

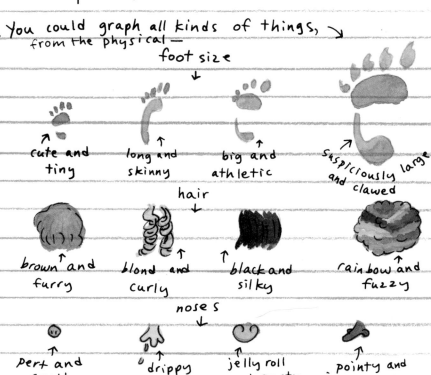

foot size ↓

↑
cute and tiny

↑
long and skinny

↑
big and athletic

↑
suspiciously large and clawed

hair ↓

↑
brown and furry

↑
blond and curly

↑
black and silky

↑
rainbow and fuzzy

noses ↓

↑
pert and small

↑
drippy and sniffly

↑
jelly roll and snorty

↑
pointy and in your business

That gave me the idea for a story.

THE TALE OF THE FEET
OR THE FOOTNOTE!

Once upon a time there was a girl who NEVER took off her shoes. Even swimming she kept them on.

Look, Ma, I can still swim.

Even with heavy feet.

Everyone thought the girl was really strange, and because she wouldn't tell why she always wore her shoes, people made up their own reasons.

1) She had ugly calluses.

2) She had gross toe gunk problems.

what you get from cramming too-big feet into too-small shoes →

← more than toe jam — it's toe crust

3) She had the smelliest feet ever.

SAVE ME!

I don't want to go NEAR those feet!

The girl heard what people said about her.

And she didn't like it one bit.

Why do you assume only bad things about my feet?

Can't people be different in a GOOD way? Are there only BAD kinds of differences?

The other kids didn't know what to say. After all, everyone was different in some way or other. But some differences were more embarrassing. Finally one kid spoke up.

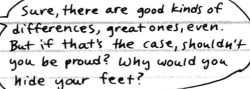

Sure, there are good kinds of differences, great ones, even. But if that's the case, shouldn't you be proud? Why would you hide your feet?

The girl thought a minute. Then very slowly and deliberately she untied her shoes. She took them off. Then she took off her socks and stood before everyone with

Wow! Amazing!

Cool!

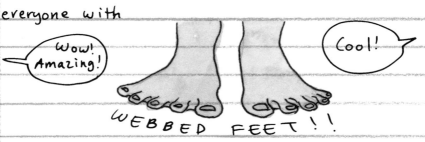

WEBBED FEET!!

Her feet weren't gross at all — they were really cool! The girl smiled. She loved the breeze tickling her toes, and the next day she wore sandals to school. Not flip-flops, of course ← She was like a whole new person — and she was definitely lighter on her toes!

Today was our last day and our last chance to try the climbing wall. I don't know why, but I heard myself saying, "C'mon, Cleo, you can do it! Go first and show everyone how it's done!"

Cleo shook her head. "I'm not ready yet. I don't want to be embarrassed two days in a row."

"What's a little embarrassment between friends?" I asked. I couldn't believe I said that — I was calling Cleo a friend! I'd NEVER done that before.

I guess she liked it, because she grinned and nodded. "Okay, here goes nothing!"

This time I was yelling with everyone else.

A wave of voices rose, pushing Cleo up, up, up. A couple of times she missed her footing, but she didn't fall and she didn't give up. She kept on going
ALL THE WAY TO THE TOP!

"You are so lucky to have her as your sister!" Sharleen said.

"See!" Carly nodded. "Cleo's not all bad. That girl has guts!"

"I know," I agreed. "I really do. Sometimes I just forget." I could see Cleo looking down and I worried she would get dizzy, maybe even throw up (that would be SO Cleo). But she kept on looking until she caught my eye. And she winked!

I couldn't help it. I yelled, "That's my sister! Way to go, Cleo!"

When Cleo got back down, a bunch of kids ran up to hug her.

I just stood and watched.

When the kids let go, Cleo walked up to me.

"Thanks, Amelia, for believing in me."

I nodded and felt my cheeks burn. Now I really was embarrassed but in a good kind of way. I felt something different, too, something I couldn't remember feeling before. I felt proud, proud of Cleo!

I stuck out my hand stiffly. "Good job, Cleo."

And we shook hands. It felt right.

I still didn't want to sit next to Cleo on the bus ride home (her queasiness hasn't changed after all), but somehow having her along wasn't as annoying as before. The whole class sang songs and took turns telling jokes and riddles. My riddle was: what's the difference between a mountain and a molehill? Answer: If you can't tell, I'm not going climbing with you!

I made it to the top!

Big deal!

Ms. Reilly couldn't resist having a captive audience (there's no escape on a bus!) so she read to us from Darwin's voyage to the Galapagos Islands on the Beagle. "Since we have this time together, we may as well learn something — right, class?"

Imagine all the snails on the Galapagos!

"Right!" we all yelled. One thing we've learned is it's better to agree with Ms. Reilly — or you'll get double the information overload.

When I got home from the school trip, the first thing I saw was a postcard from Nadia waiting for me. ↓

Dear Amelia,
  I know it's hard to get out from under Cleo's shadow, but you'll just have to make your own shadow, if you know what I mean. People have to judge you for who you are, not who Cleo is. If they don't, that's their loss. Your friends don't think of you like that. Do the others really matter?
  Anyway, I'm sure it won't be the most embarrassing field trip of your life. Remember the one to the jelly bean factory?

luv, Nadia   yours till the ink blots

23¢

sitting pretty

Amelia
564 North Homerest
Oopa, Oregon
97881

As usual, she's right, even more right than she thinks. I've got to start seeing Cleo for who she is, just like I want people to see me. And I'm NOT going to be embarrassed by her anymore. She can embarrass herself all she wants, but from now on I'm in charge of my own embarrassing moments. I'm sure I'll have enough without taking on hers as well! And I don't have to let her cast a shadow over me. I'm standing in the sun, no matter what — with my shoes off and proud of it!

I forgot about pulling that lever and pouring 68 pounds of jelly beans all over the floor! That's a great story to tell! Next time...

This book is dedicated to Ruth Heller,
who was too gracious to get embarrassed, no matter what!

Look! He's blushing! ⟶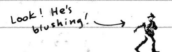

SIMON & SCHUSTER BOOKS FOR YOUNG READERS
An imprint of Simon & Schuster Children's Publishing Division
1230 Avenue of the Americas, New York, New York 10020

A Paula Wiseman Book

SIMON & SCHUSTER BOOKS FOR YOUNG READERS
is a trademark of Simon & Schuster, Inc.

Book design by Amelia
(with help from Lucy Ruth Cummins) ← Thanks!

The text for this book is hand-lettered. ↖ All spelling mistakes are embarrassingly my own!

Manufactured in China 1210 KWO
6   8   10   9   7

Library of Congress Cataloging-in-Publication Data
Moss, Marissa
Amelia's most unforgettable embarrassing moments / Marissa Moss.—1st ed.
p. cm.
ISBN 0-689-87041-8 (ISBN-13: 978-0-689-87041-5)
Amelia records in her diary a nightmare come true when
her older sister tags along on a sixth-grade class trip,
and Amelia must deal with snoring and disgusting
eating habits. [1. Sisters—Fiction. 2. Embarrassment—
Fiction. 3. School field trips—Fiction. 4. Diaries—
Fiction.] I. Title.

PZ7. M8535Alu2005
[Fic]—dc22
2004059006